STEAL THE BACON

Johns Hopkins: Poetry and Fiction
John T. Irwin, General Editor

Guy Davenport, *Da Vinci's Bicycle: Ten Stories*
John Hollander, *"Blue Wine" and Other Poems*
Robert Pack, *Waking to My Name: New and Selected Poems*
Stephen Dixon, *Fourteen Stories*
Philip Dacey, *The Boy under the Bed*
Jack Matthews, *Dubious Persuasions*
Guy Davenport, *Tatlin!*
Wyatt Prunty, *The Times Between*
Barry Spacks, *Spacks Street: New and Selected Poems*
Joe Ashby Porter, *The Kentucky Stories*
Gibbons Ruark, *Keeping Company*
Stephen Dixon, *Time to Go*
Jack Matthews, *Crazy Women*
David St. John, *Hush*
Jean McGarry, *Airs of Providence*
Wyatt Prunty, *What Women Know, What Men Believe*
Adrien Stoutenberg, *Land of Superior Mirages:*
    New and Selected Poems
John Hollander, *In Time and Place*
Jack Matthews, *Ghostly Populations*
Charles Martin, *Steal the Bacon*
Jean McGarry, *The Very Rich Hours*

STEAL THE BACON

Charles Martin

The Johns Hopkins University Press

BALTIMORE AND LONDON

This book has been brought to publication with
the generous assistance of the G. Harry Pouder Fund
and the Albert Dowling Trust.

The Johns Hopkins University Press
701 West 40th Street
Baltimore, Maryland 21211
The Johns Hopkins Press Ltd., London

The paper used in this publication meets the
minimum requirements of American National Standard
for Information Sciences—Permanence of Paper for
Printed Library Materials, ANSI Z39.48-1984.

Library of Congress Cataloging-in-Publication Data

Martin, Charles, 1942–
  Steal the bacon.

  (Johns Hopkins, poetry and fiction)
  I. Title. II. Series.
PS3563.A72327S7 1987   811'.54   86-46285
ISBN 0-8018-3493-7 (alk. paper)
ISBN 0-8018-3494-5 (pbk.: alk. paper)

for Greg and Emily
the story is clearly meant for the girl and boy

Contents

Acknowledgments   XI

Complaint of the Night Watchman   XIII

I FROM THE NESTING PLACE

Steal the Bacon   3

After the Rape of the Sabine Women   5

Design   6

A Burial at Shanidar   7

Domestic Interior   9

Speech against Stone   10

Rough Draft   12

The Housatonic at Falls Village   13

On Yielding to Whim   14

Metaphor of Grass in California   15

A Happy Ending for the Lost Children   16

II PASSAGES FROM FRIDAY

E.S.L.   21

Passages from Friday   24

Mr Dorrington's Discovery   49

III LANDSCAPE WITHOUT HISTORY

Easter Sunday, 1985   53

July 1914   54

"Grace, Secrets, Mysteries . . . "   56

Mandelstam in Transit   58

Landscape without History   59

To the Living Bait   63

Making Faces   65

Acknowledgments

Some poems in this volume appeared in the following periodicals, to whose editors grateful acknowledgment is made: *Boulevard:* "Design," "A Burial at Shanidar," "Metaphor of Grass in California," "Easter Sunday, 1985"; *Chronicle:* "Making Faces"; *Cumberland Poetry Review:* "July 1914," "Mandelstam in Transit"; *Hudson Review:* "Speech against Stone," "'Grace, Secrets, Mysteries . . . '"; *Inquiry:* "After the Rape of the Sabine Women"; *Little Magazine:* "To the Living Bait"; *Nebo:* "Complaint of the Night Watchman"; *New England Review and Bread Loaf Quarterly:* "Three Passages from Friday"; *The New Yorker:* "The Housatonic at Falls Village"; *Ontario Review:* "A Happy Ending for the Lost Children," "Landscape without History"; *Orpheus:* "Rough Draft"; and *Threepenny Review:* "Steal the Bacon."

The poems in section two first appeared in a limited-edition chapbook, *Passages from Friday,* published by Abattoir Editions.

I am grateful to the trustees of the Ingram Merrill Foundation for a grant that aided me in writing many of the poems in this book.

I would like to thank the trustees of the Djerassi Foundation for residencies that greatly aided me in completing this book.

Complaint of the Night Watchman

The tower they are building turns to speech,
Narrows almost to nowhere, nearing completion.
The builders have no grasp of their tower's reach
And more fall silent as each new addition
Leaves them all left with less and less to stand on,
Becoming fictions with each winding story.
It wasn't this that the builders had planned on
When they imagined for themselves the glory
Of this unparalleled erection, a tower
That would rise to heaven, making man divine.
But they ignored or perhaps had forgotten the power
That merely human speech has to undermine
Godlike achievement. Grave misapprehension:
Now word of Babel—that is their name for it—
Flies on the four winds, and every vagrant mention
Brings news of their inflated claim for it
To heaven, where this pleases not at all.
The gods confer about this grand delusion.
They do so even now. It must soon fall,
And those who'd build it fall into confusion
Of language, and the race of builders scatter.
With them will go odd pieces of the rubble
To stand for failed unity. And of more matter,
Tongues that will turn their failure into fable.

I

FROM THE NESTING PLACE

Steal the Bacon

"First Flossie . . . then Sean . . . and now Moe. . . . " Surely
   their brightest
Are bright enough to have already noticed
That every morning the one who last molded elastic
Bones and went pouring like mercury under
The molding does not return. Surely someone must wonder,
"What in God's name ever becomes of them?"
Trap crushes snout and hind legs tap out a spastic
Coda, diminuendo, on cold linoleum,

Far from the muzzy warmth of the nest, that supportive
   nexus
Of sensual mouselife. Those are x's
That were his eyes, or hers. And doesn't anyone notice
A cherished aunt or uncle's sudden
Vanishing act? "Let's see now . . . Flossie disappeared one
Night last week . . . was she the first? Was Sean?
Mousebrain! Why can't I keep them in order? I only know
   this:
That one by one we seem to be drawn

Forward against our wills, tho' scampering brightly
Toward that narrow strip of light we
All of us fear. Beyond it, the high kitchen table;
Delectable odors that overcome Reason
And Prudence; blistery fragments of grilled cheese on
Stale crust; and the fatty bacon
That somehow kills, in the legend which is, whether fact or
   fable,
The nightmare from which we would awaken. . . . "

Real mice in silence rise to the subtly baited
Trap not caring whether free or fated.
Springy gray squealers pulse with indecision,
Wrinkling their vulnerable noses
As they try to answer the question this poised engine poses.
And then either scamper back under the wall
Or stay to play steal the bacon—a game in which steely
    precision
Cracks down on mouseflesh or down on nothing at all.

After the Rape of the Sabine Women

They never speak of what happened during their capture,
The house-to-house searches, the violent seizures,
The brisk allotment of women to sausage-faced soldiers
Ripping off bronze-plated armor in innocent rapture:
But of some last choice made earlier that morning,
The lover or book chosen for wit, for beauty
Or for idleness torn out of hand without warning
And flung away broken. Now, in the streets of the city,
They move with an air of abstraction, pushing their infants
Before them, like so many dowsers searching for water;
Breasts drip with milk, knuckles whiten on a stroller's
Chromium bar: a single moment's confusion
Leaves one a hostage forever, inscribing invisible,
Momentary lines in the language of desire.

Design

Lines scored across this fragment of a bone
Worked by a smaller piece of sharpened stone

Gripped firmly in a hand now dust may tell
How to apportion time or cast a spell;

But whether they were calendar or curse,
The scratched recording of some deathless verse

Or none of the above, we cannot say:
Can only say the readings that we take

Of this now enigmatic instrument
Indicate aim, purpose, some meaning meant—

Meaning, in this case, goes against the grain,
Would not be noticed otherwise. Design,

Whether we find it legible or not,
Reveals itself in what is taken out,

A kind of absence in a thing designed
By which we recognize the presence of mind.

A Burial at Shanidar

Men of our kind digging in the cellar
Of a cave uncovered what was hidden:
Bones that from steeping in the earth's strong tea
Had long since taken on its color.
But were those bones just tossed onto the midden,
Or had they been buried? A mystery.
The soiled fragments of a salvaged skull
At first said nothing but Neanderthal.

Bones in better repair, found underneath
That skull's dyed egg, proclaimed themselves to be
Those of an old man crippled by arthritis,
An old man of forty, arthritic since birth,
A burden on the group. And yet, improbably,
They had provided for him in his lifetime
And afterwards had put him in the ground
With ceremony, as our cave men found.

For when they sent the matter of that site
To be examined by a botanist
In Europe, she at once discovered
The remnants of a grave—a shallow pit
Lined with pine branches to make a place
To which the corpse was borne, on which it was covered
With what could not have gotten there by chance:
Cornflowers, hollyhock, grape-hyacinth.

Custom revealed in the dried-out pollen
Of flowers now nothing dropped by hands of no
More substance now than the shadows on the wall
That flickered in firelight when one by one
They came forward in hesitant slow
Motion to attend that funeral—
Those dim, unsightly ancestors of ours,
Each one clutching a spray of wildflowers,

Uttering their little cries of unsuccess,
Almost human enough to seem grotesque
As they approach the figure in the grave;
Each one mumbling what might have meant, Take these,
Which we have gathered at no little risk
In the wild places far beyond the cave.
We thought to honor you.
                              The reasons why
Would perish with the last of them to die.

Domestic Interior

Whenever I try to imagine the Garden
Of Eden, I see an upended cave
Like the one which my son has created
Out of the now lidless cardboard carton
In which a neighbor's Frigidaire arrived;
And an old woollen blanket, liberated
From an upstairs closet. Done with the chore
Of rearranging mental furniture,

He clambers into his place and hunkers down
Among the odors, those imaginary
Friends from an unimaginable past;
Warmed by his warmth, they come forth, voices drawn
Out of the blanket's faded memory,
Out of the threadbare fabric of that nest.

Speech against Stone

I watch the man in the schoolyard
As he brushes a flat coat of institutional beige
Over a wall brilliant with childish graffiti,
      Turning a fresh page,

A surface the kids will respray
As soon as his back is turned. I suppose I should
Be thinking—as any upstanding, taxpay-
      ing citizen would—

Of the money and man-hours spent
Covering up these phosphorescent hues
And adolescent cries of discontent;
      But as he continues,

I find myself divided:
The huge roller goes sweeping on over the stone,
And I see in what he is doing a labor
      Not unlike my own

When I erase, letter by letter,
The words I've just written, in the hope that all
My scratching out may summon something better—
      And besides, the wall

Surely approves of this work,
For who can believe that it would choose to say
FUCK THE WORLD or FAT ANTHONYS A JERK
      Or DMF JOSE?

No, left to its own devices,
The wall would stand forever an unlettered book,
Prepared to meet eternity's inspection
   With its own blank look.

But that, of course, is what summons
The hidden children out of their hiding places—
That inviting blankness as the janitor finally covers
   Up the last traces,

Gathers together his painting
Gear and goes clattering off. No sooner gone
Than they return to renew the ancient complaint
   Of speech against stone,

Spelling out—misspelling, often—
The legends of the heart's lust for joy and violence
In waves that break upon but will not soften
   The cliffs of obdurate silence.

Rough Draft

Popping gum, cracking wise,
At poolside she defies
Gravity: lifted in her not quite skin-
tight pink maillol, she shrieks uproar-
iously as the boyfriend starts to spin
Her across one brawny shoulder:

No Rogers, no Astaire:
Her legs scissor the air
With an unglamorously panicked glee,
And he's too stocky and too short
For idoldom: set down, she lurches free:
Her taunting cry, his low retort:

Ignoring the cold print
Forbidding it, they sprint
Outrageously around the pool: arrive
In a final burst of laughter
At the deep end: turn without pause and dive
Into enveloping water:

Explode at the other
End, breathless, together.
Dripping, subdued, they recompose themselves
And then go walking off. Traces
Of a distant light lie broken on the waves
Their passage scribbles and erases.

The Housatonic at Falls Village

I MARRIAGE

In a landscape of abstractions, it has its place.
The carp have been abstracted from the water,
The carp lie weeping in their wicker basket.
They are weeping for marriage and for divorce,
For the clear jelly that holds the roe together
And for the smoky pulse of milt that quickens and scatters;
For the bright hook dancing its doughball
In front of their bobbling lips.
                             In the windy sunlight,
The numberless hinges of their bodies stiffen.

II ROMANCE

It too has its place: here, where the others
Are always absent at just the right moment,
A waterfall etches its acids into gray rock
Strewn with the threat of copperheads—dull somniacs
Pouring like honey from one ledge to another.
Are they calligraphy or parable? A diver
Scales the steep face of the cliff to its summit,
Turns, and then folds himself cleanly into the water.

On Yielding to Whim

for D.G., *someone*
raised in a landscape short of rain

Someone imagines that he sees a cat
Crouching in these hot hills—another burns
For the lounging odalisk which he discerns
Couched in the same duncolored folds of what
Is, underneath, mere stone—despite its range
Of attitudes, characters, reveries. . . .
Two of the nearer hills, encouraged, rise
Slowly and languorously stretching change

Into a form made of the appetite
To find a form there, let the mind's eye trace
Imaginary lines to metaphor—
A cat? A woman? A moment and no more:
Mirages ordinary to a place
Stingy with water, generous with light.

Metaphor of Grass in California

The seeds of certain grasses that once grew
Over the graves of those who fell at Troy
Were brought to California in the hooves
Of Spanish cattle. Trodden into the soil,

They liked it well enough to germinate,
Awakening into another scene
Of conquest: blade fell upon flashing blade
Until the native grasses fled the field,

And the native flowers bowed to their dominion.
Small clumps of them fought on as they retreated
Toward isolated ledges of serpentine,
Repellent to their conquerors. . . .
                              In defeat,

They were like men who see their city taken,
And think of grass—how soon it will conceal
All of the scattered bodies of the slain;
As such men fall, these fell, but silently.

A Happy Ending for the Lost Children

One of their picture books would no doubt show
The two lost children wandering in a maze
Of anthropomorphic tree limbs: the familiar crow

Swoops down upon the trail they leave of corn,
Tolerant of the error of their ways.
Hand in hand they stumble onto the story,

Brighteyed with beginnings of fever, scared
Half to death, yet never for a moment
Doubting the outcome that had been prepared

Long in advance: Girl saves brother from oven,
Appalling witch dies in appropriate torment;
Her hoarded treasure buys them their parents' love.

       *   *   *

"As happy an ending as any fable
Can provide," squawks the crow, who had expected more:
Delicate morsels from the witch's table.

It's an old story—in the modern version
The random children fall to random terror.
You see it nightly on the television:

Cameras focus on the lopeared bear
Beside the plastic ukulele, shattered
In a fit of rage—the lost children are

Found in the first place we now think to look:
Under the fallen leaves, under the scattered
Pages of a lost childrens' picture book.

       *   *   *

But if we leave terror waiting in the rain
For the wrong bus, or if we have terror find,
At the very last moment the right train,

Only to get off at the wrong station—
If we for once imagine a happy ending,
Which is, as always, a continuation,

It's because the happy ending's a necessity,
It isn't just a sentimental ploy—
Without the happy ending there would be

No one to tell the story to but the witch,
And the story is clearly meant for the girl and boy
Just now about to step into her kitchen.

II

Passages from Friday

E. S. L.

My frowning students carve
Me monsters out of prose:
This one—a gargoyle—thumbs its contemptuous nose
At how, in English, subject must agree
With verb—for any such agreement shows
   Too great a willingness to serve,
      A docility

   Which wiry Miss Choi
   Finds un-American.
She steals a hard look at me. I wink. Her grin
Is my reward. *In his will, our peace, our Pass:*
Gargoyle erased, subject and verb now in
   Agreement, reach object, enjoy
      Temporary truce.

   Tonight my students must
   Agree or disagree:
America is still a land of opportunity.
The answer is always, uniformly, *Yes*—even though
"It has no doubt that here were to much free,"
   As Miss Torrico will insist.
      She and I both know

   That Language binds us fast,
   And those of us without
Are bound and gagged by those within. Each fledgling
     polyglot
Must shake old habits: tapping her sneakered feet,
Miss Choi exorcises incensed ancestors, flout-
   ing the ghosts of her Chinese past.
      Writhing in the seat

Next to Miss Choi, Mister
Fedakis, in anguish
Labors to express himself in a tongue which
Proves *Linear B* to me, when I attempt to read it
Later. They're here for English as a Second Language,
  Which I'm teaching this semester.
    God knows they need it,

  And so, thank God, do they.
  The night's made easier
By our agreement: I am here to help deliver
Them into the good life they write me papers about.
English is pre-requisite for that endeavor,
  Explored in their nightly essays
    Boldly setting out

  To reconnoiter the fair
  New World they would enter:
Suburban Paradise, the endless shopping center
Where one may browse for hours before one chooses
Some new necessity—gold-flecked magenta
  Wallpaper to re-do the spare
    Bath no one uses,

  Or a machine which can,
  In seven seconds, crush
A newborn calf into such seamless mush
As a *mousse* might be made of—or our true sublime:
The gleaming counters where frosted cosmeticians brush
  Decades from the allotted span,
    Abrogating Time

As the spring tide brushes
    A single sinister
Footprint from the otherwise unwrinkled shore
Of America the Blank. In absolute confusion
Poor Mister Fedakis rumbles with despair
    And puts the finishing smutches
        To his conclusion

    While Miss Choi erases:
    One more gargoyle routed.
Their pure, erroneous lines yield an illuminated
Map of the new found land. We will never arrive there,
Since it exists only in what we say about it,
    As all the rest of my class is
        Bound to discover.

Passages from Friday

In a little Time, I began to speak
to him, and teach him to speak to me;
having sav'd him on the 6th Day of the Week,
I made him know that his Name was to be

Friday; *I thought it right to call him so*
for the Memory of the Time; in the same Way
I taught him to say Master, *then let him know*
from this Day on, that was to be my Name.

With my owne thoro' un-Worthyness
all Ways befor my Face I turn to
this burthensom Task which nevertheless
being decided, *Viz.* That I must learn to

write as my *Master* did & so set down
tho' withowt any Hope of Recovery
from this inchanted Island to my owne
Nation whence taken in Captivity

som Yeers a go: That by the diligent
copying of Letters from his Bokes
now my owne I ha' further'd this Intent
to sutch Degree wher all most now it looks

if I may say so now it makes me think
that Heaven smiles upon my Enterprise:
That having got a Quantity of Ink
at no great Cost express'd from native Berries

sutch as may express my Native Wit
most suitably, if I may so conceive:
That having obtain'd sutch Fethers as are fit
to write with, once sharpen'd, I will now leave

all mis-givings as to my Ability
& here invoke all-mighty *Providence:*
That having from my *Master* a Supply
of What to write on, I will now commence

with an Accownt of my Deliverance
as this commenc'd my *new* or 2nd Life;
for, being ignorant of *Providence*
& its Design, I cling'd to the Belief

that thos seiz'd in War-fare cou'd be eaten;
this, I had learn'd, was what my *God* intended:
So, when my owne Nation was defeated
& I took Prisoner, it seem'd my Life was ended;

truss'd up & cast into a War-*Canoo*
I lay as one all ready Dead & thought
ownly of, *What my Enemy wou'd do.*
Soon as this Island I was abruptly brought

to Sacrifice, as one by 1 my 3
Fellowes were knock'd down, cut open & burn'd:
One still a live, twisting so in Agony
that it a mews'd my Captor, the Fellow turn'd

to watch the Sport: Up I leap & race
as swiftly as I can a long the Shoar:
A Cry goes up: Two of my Foes give Chace:
I run from them till I can run no more

when suddenly a Cross my Path ther flies
what seems a Mountain, cover'd all in Hair!
I tumble Grownd-ward, a trembling with Surprise:
Have I escap'd the Snell but for the Snare?

This *Mountain* proves *Volcano,* belching Fire
that strikes the foremost of my Persuers Dead
at which the 2nd one runs off in Terror;
I place the *Masters* Foot upon my Head.

II

My Beginning begun, I must begin agayn
for, tho' my *Master* is no longer a live,
his Spirit guides the Movement of my Pen
a Cross this Sheet, commanding me: *To give*

*a true Account of owr Life together
in all Particulars:* How each Day was spent
from 1st Light, when I go off to gather
Fewel for the Fire lay'd owt Side his Tent

then fetch his Cloathes for him & lay them owt:
Then leve him be now: Run off to prepare
his Goats-Flesh Stewe; this done, I hear him showt:
Bring him his Jugg: I fetch it in & pour

him a great Supp to drink, whilst he dresses
& then attend him till his Stewe is eaten
& then if all has not been as he pleases
as like as not poor *Friday* will get beaten;

then off to tend the Flock whos swolne Dams
bleating together urgently complain
of my Neglect; an Howre on my Hams
& thence to gather up what Scraps remain

after my *Master;* next to weed the Corn
which occupies my Time befor his Dinner
must be prepar'd; so passes the Morn;
It is because poor Friday *is a Sinner*

that he must spend his Days Gain-fully toiling,
my *Master* tells me; I slice his Bread & Chees
& bast with Grees the Joynt of Goat-Flesh broiling;
whil he has Dinner, *Friday* takes his Ease.

The after Noon was spent a frighting Game;
Parots especially he lov'd to kill,
for, having taught i once to say his Name,
that one, escaping, had pass'd on the Skill

to others of the brightly Fether'd Race;
so then, wherever in the Woods we go
from Tree to Tree a Head of us they chace
crying, *Robinson   Robinson   Crusoe*

Heedless of wasted Powder when he's vext
he fires off his Peeces 1 by 1
whil *Parots* fly from one Tree to the next
crying, *Crusoe   Crusoe   Robinson*

III

I mind 1 Time we bilded us a Raft
which, he say'd was, *A Work of no little Art;*
but the Islands Magick overcame his Craft
& the first Tide that took it, shook it a Part

& left the Peeces scatter'd on the Shoar;
for the Island held him firmly in its Grip
& wou'd not let go. It was not long befor
he had a nother Plan: *We wou'd bild a Ship*

owt of a hallow'd Log. Weeks must be spent
in searching of the Mountains for a Tree
that wou'd, in all Things, answer his Intent;
at last we found owr Selves a *Mahagonny*

which, he was sure, wou'd serve his Purpose well.
I guess'd it wou'd not, for when we found it
This Tree commenc'd groaning; when we began to fell
the lesser Trees that grew up all a round it

thes groan'd as well; I hear'd, but *Master* cou'd not;
earnestly I begg'd him, *To find a nother*
Tree, but he was adamant & wou'd not
hear of sutch Talk; a Cuffing for my Bother.

Now after we had cleer'd a Way the Grownd
came the felling of this prodigious Tree
no Tree at all, but a Womans Spryght imprison'd
which, as we cut it, moan'd so piteously

that owr Axes were enchanted by
the Sownd to sutch Degree that they lept back
in owr Hands, *as tho' they'd rather try
owr Flesh than hers.* After 1 sutch Attack

I saw that *Master* had been somewhat nick'd
by my owne Blade, which I at once let go;
I seiz'd his wounded Hand in mine & lick'd
the Blood a Way, as any Man wou'd do

owt of meer Affection; he wrenches loos
his Hand from mine & violently throes
me to the Grownd with scurrilous Abuse
& drives me from him with repeated Kicks & Blows.

IV

An Howre every Evening was given
to my Instruction, by which, however
imperfectly, I learn'd of *Hell & Heaven,*
the *Middle Way,* the *Pulley* & the *Lever*

& many a nother Use-full Invention,
astownding to me, who had mis-understood
so mutch befor; I soon form'd the Intention
of becoming as like my *Master* as I cou'd,

putting the *Cannibal* of earlier Yeers
behind me; and yet, my owne Ignorance
both hinder'd me & rais'd my *Masters* Fears
of my Savage Nature. *This* Callibans

a Canniball, he'd say: *No teaching him.*
Nevertheless, I learn'd how *God* and the *Devill*
must wage continuous War-Fare till the End of Time
or thenabowts, when *God* will putt an End to Evil;

& how to load & fire Fowling-Peeces
& cleen them after-ward; and how to cloathe
my self in Goat-Skins & to make Cheeses
from the Goats-Milk; and so on & so forth;

untill so mutch of what my *Master* knew,
I knew as well, quickly comprehending
even the meaner Things he taught me to do,
(Viz.) *cooking, cleaning-up, sewing & mending;*

and yet, tho' I did all I cou'd to plees,
learning to do & doing all I learn'd,
his Melancholy seem'd ownly to increes,
as tho' in his Innards a low Feaver burn'd.

V

When the Moons Light pours a Cross my Window-Sill
I spread my Writing owt upon my Knees
losing my Self for Howres in it till
my Wick of Oakum sputters in its Grees

& I nodd off. I had fell to dreaming
of once, when I, return'd to the Plantation
with Raizins for his Wine, I hear'd him screaming
as tho' persu'd by the whol *Caribb* Nation;

I rush'd froward, determin'd either to aid
him in his Struggle, or to fall besyde;
no one a peer'd to be at the Stockade
when I paws'd ther breefly for a Look inside;

rather I found him wher the Beasts were penn'd
& they all murther'd. He had slyt ther Throats
& as they twitch'd & skitter'd on the Grownd
he hack'd & slash'd at thes poor harm-less Goats

then order'd me to, *Bild a great big Fire;*
Naught may be sav'd of them at all, he say'd;
Let Flames consume ther Carckasses entire.
Now many of these Beasts were scarsly Dead

& others, all tho' dismember'd, still liv'd;
yet in my Fear, I none the less obey'd him,
sutch whippings & picklings as I receiv'd
whenever I objected or gainsay'd him.

Later, he say'd that the Goats had learn'd his Name
by listening to the escap'd *Parots*
& wou'd repeat it, braying, for a Game
till he was phrenzied. I say it was Spirits

that wait a bowt a Man to do him Harm
when they are able; thes infest the Island.
The Beasts being burn'd, he became quite calm
& for 3 Days remain'd a Loan in Silence.

When he came forth he went to the ruin'd Pen
& cast the Spirits owt in Peels of Laughter,
till at the last, he seem'd him-self agayn;
yet never wou'd he speak a bowt this after.

VI

But I digress here, having yet to tell
of, How we got the Tree down for owr *Canoo;*
after a whil, I offer'd to cast a Spell
to quieten the Womans Spirit, who

dwelt within it; I did a little Dance
& sprinkl'd the Grownd a round the Tree with Grain
mix'd with some Blood; the Spryght fell into Silence
& owr Axe-Blades obey'd us once agayn.

Master pretended not to see this at all
untill I had finish'd. We girdl'd it a round
then left it to bleed & dry; after severall
Weeks we came back & brought it to the Grownd.

Painfull Labour follow'd, for we must peel
all of the Bark a Way; then burn & scrape
the In-sides off with glowing Coals untill
it was hallow'd owt; then we must shape

the Out-side Part; and all of the Work we did,
owr endless toiling & incessant Care
serv'd only to show, *the Woman that was hid;*
at last her Figur was brought owt so cleer

that *Master* saw her, as he him-self confess'd;
and none of owr toiling cou'd efface
1 single Curve of Belly, Thigh or Breast.
I judg'd her to be a Woman of my Race

by Virtue of her Colour, dark as the Grayn
of that *Mahagonee* in which we found her.
Perhaps she too was brought here to be slayn
& had escap'd when her Captors unbound her

for a Moment; and running off as I did,
but finding no *Master,* no Deliverance
from her persuing Enemies, she hid
her-self by taking leave of her Womans

Body & becoming at once a meer Tree;
her Roots sunk down, her Branches lifted high,
she blossom'd into a Security
that lasted untill we 2 hapn'd by.

VII

Of thos sever'd Branches I mutch later made
my *European Figur Fetisches,*
7 in Number, painted & array'd
a long the Shoar to ward off Savages

& to attrackt thos Shipps I some Times spy'd
at a great Distance; but they never came neer
all tho' at some Times the Savages did,
when, after War-fare they brought Captives heer

to feast upon them. I some Times discover'd
Remainders of ther Feasts upon the Sand
or in it, when my prodding Toe uncover'd
an eyeless Skull, a blackned Foot or Hand;

ther were 7 of thes Figurs, as I say'd;
and all of them stood facing owt to Sea
with Musket in one Hand & a naked Blade
in the other, scowling ferociously.

Often I try'd, but never succeeded,
in a wakening them; that Enterprise
was doom'd, for What my Europeans needed
was not my dancing, but a Shipps Supplies;

more Hats & Cloathes & shiny buckl'd Shoes,
more Axes, Muskets, Cannon & Gun-Powder,
more of sutch Goods than they cou'd ever use;
ownly sutch Abundance cou'd have rows'd them.

I danc'd abowt & summon'd them to dance
but they ignor'd my importunate Commotion;
fix'd in ther Places as tho' in a Trance,
staring with painted Eyes at the great Ocean.

VIII

My *Masters* Plan was this: Ther was a Stream
I hundred Yards or so up-Hill of owr
Camp; in the rainy Season, it became
a raging Torrent, into which we'd lower

owr *Peragua,* as he lik'd to call it;
and let that Torrent bring it down to Sea.
I ask'd him, *How we wou'd ever haul it
thos hundred Yards?* He answer'd, *I wou'd be*

*a Beast of Burthen, which do not complayn
no Matter how heavy the Tasks theyr made to do;*
he wou'd be likewise, for, *Who grutches Pain
that have at last Deliverance in View?*

And so we begun. Despite his good Intent
the Labour was inequally divided:
Whenever Shoulders were needed, *Fridays* bent;
whenever Decisions, *Master* decided.

Rollers were cut & lay'd a long the Grownd
a Part of the Way, and the *Canoo* was hoist
upon them: Ropes from her Bow were run a round
a Windlass, which my *Master* had devis'd;

and when we turn'd this Windless, owr *Canoo*
seem'd to a waken; it shudder'd & groan'd
& slid upon thes Rollers for a few
Yards at a Time, till owr Rope was wound

a round the Windlass; or the Rope broke through;
or the Wind-less broke down; or a Roller slid
owt of the Way & stranded the *Canoo;*
or, if som other Thing cou'd fail, it did:

for nothing he ever did was done with Ease
of Natur; for, according to *Providence,*
all Things had Value ownly from ther *Use,*
& had no *Feelings* nor *Intelligence,*

which we call *Spirit;* and which they did withowt;
he call'd me *Savage,* that I cou'd not see
how Things were Tools & how thes Tools allow'd
us to master mor Things: For it appear'd to me

that it was them that master'd us; by making
us work so mutch for What we little needed;
and, when we wanted them, by all Ways breaking;
so that they labour'd rather less than we did.

IX

It took 2 Months befor we reach'd the Stream,
but we were not yet done; *Master* intended,
That the *Canoo* must be slung owt in between
2 opposing Trees, hoist up & suspended

over the Creek, that, once the Flood began
she cou'd be launch'd withowt being swept a Way;
had all Things hapned according to his Plan—
but that they did not, I scarsly need say.

We got the Boat slung in betwixt the Trees
& hoist her up; and then went back to move
owr Camp to the Creek; and then took owr Ease,
he in a Tent & I in the *Canoo,*

which, like a Hammock, lull'd me into Slumber;
I saw my Self (cradl'd in my Dream
by yeelding Flesh, not by unyeelding Timber)
sleeping once mor in my owne Mothers Womb,

as in the Waters under-neath the Earth;
I felt her Body shuddering & trembling
& knew that soon I wou'd be dropp'd in Birth;
and in my Ears hear'd a thund'rous rumbling

which suddenly stopp'd: Now I hear'd someone call
my Name, and sitting up, saw my *Master* drench'd
upon the Bank, poynting to the Wattery Wall
that, at the next Moment, crash'd on me & launch'd

owr *Canoo* onto the swolne River
with me In-side it; tho' not, I fear'd, for long;
as the *Canoo,* a Log once more, roll'd over
& whipp'd a bowt, was taken up & flung

now heer, now ther, now up & now below,
compell'd to dance the Rivers merry Dance;
I griev'd for my *Master,* losing at one Blow
his ownly Servant & his Deliverance,

& shed more Tears for him, than for my Self.
What hapned after this was Wonder-full:
As in my Dream, Wood melted into Flesh
& a warm Hand press'd me to the Hull

a Hull no longer: For the Flood releas'd
the Woman that was hid in the *Canoo*
& with me clinging tightly to her Waist
she swum & frollick'd like a *Whale* or *Sea-Cow;*

I was no longer affraid now of Death,
tho' we dove down Water-Falls immensly high
into the deep Pools that had form'd beneath,
then let the Current take us by & by

the 2 of us at one with the Water
& she cavorting in it merrily
& the arch'd Trees echoing with her Laughter:
As *Dolphins* carry Children, she carry'd me,

my Arms & Legs secure a bowt her fastned:
When she roll'd over on her Belly, I twin'd her
Hair in my Hands
                    great Coils of black Hair glisten'd
like *Water-Serpents* streaming owt behind her

X

When *Master* found me at the Streams Embouchure
his Joy in finding that I had not dy'd
seem'd nicely balanc'd by his Discomfiture;
at first kissing & embraceing me, he cry'd

Thou art a live why then I'm not a Loan;
but then his Smiles were driven off by Tears:
O wher has the Hope of my Deliverance gone?
He thwack'd & pummel'd me a bowt the Ears

untill his Arms, exhausted by this Game,
sank to his Sides and he sunk down be Side
me on the Sand wher I'd sank down the same
& then embrac'd me once more & once more cry'd

but beat on me no more. We stay'd like that
for quite a whil, and then he ask'd, *What hapned
to his* Canoo? *Was it stove in or what?*
I told him all that I ha' just now written

except for, What he had all ready seen,
viz, how it broak a Way; but I told him how
it chang'd into the Woman who had been
trapp'd in the Tree, *et cetera;* and how

she carry'd me, once she had gotten owt,
down the whol River, till we came at length
to where he found me, by the Rivers Mouth;
to all of which he listen'd to in Silence,

nodding his Head ownly, a little Bit;
so I went on further, telling him of my
Distress, when I gather'd that she meant to quit
the Island all together, seeing that I

must choose betwicks my *Freedom* & my *Master*,
to whom I ow'd so mutch; here, *Master* nodded:
Lengthening her Stroaks, she swum mutch faster,
heading Sea-ward; till I cry'd owt & prodded

her Flanks with my Toes to-wards the Island;
then she roll'd over on her Back & pick'd me up
& look'd at me for a great long Whil and
smil'd at me, *as at a poor, bedraggl'd Pup,*

for sutch I must ha' seem'd to her no Doubt;
then dropp'd me in be-Side her, and with the Palm
of her Hand, gave me a Push; I struck owt
for the Island, and in a little Whil I'd swum

back to the Rivers Mowth; once safely a Shoar
I try'd to spot her, but she had disappear'd,
and I never saw that Woman any more,
and so I lay down, being suddenly tir'd.

Master say'd nothing, when I was all done,
but meerly sat with his Chin upon his Breast
staring with Eyes vacant of Expression:
When I ask'd him, *If he did not wish to rest,*

he rose & totter'd off on down the Beach;
when he return'd, he had in Hand a few
Peeces of Wood which he had found & which
he say'd was from the broaken-up *Canoo;*

Not possible, says I; but he ignor'd
my owne Account, as, *It did not make Sense:*
Why, no sutch Thing as that never occur'd,
Or wou'd I mock both him & Providence?

XI

At first I little thought how hard my *Master*
took the Loss of owr *Peragua-Canoo;*
but it prov'd, as he say'd, ı *Disaster*
too many for him: That, having gone thro'

sutch a vast Labour of ungrutching Pain
& when Deliverance was near on Hand
to have his bright Hopes extinguish'd by the Rain:
Why, this was too mutch for any Man to stand,

He'd say, shaking his Head in Dis-belief.
And after this, he grew Absent in his Mind,
talking to him-self, mainly, and wandering off
into the Woods with his Jugg of Raisin Wine.

One Evening an Accident occur'd
which left him neer Dead, tho' not entirely:
whil I was cleaning up, he disappear'd,
taking a long his Jugg for Company;

he must ha' wander'd for a good long Time,
pawsing every now & agayn for a Swig;
soon good & lost, he must ha' try'd to climb
a Hill to get his Bearings; but he & the Jugg,

with him half-fill'd & it half-empty, spill'd
down a steep Sloap untill a scrubby Oak
shatter'd the one & very nearly kill'd
the other; inducing in him sutch a Stroak

as left him helpless. When I reach'd him, he
lay withowt moving & ownly roll'd his Eyes
a round his Head as tho' beseeching me
for some Thing or other; but other Wise

he was incapable of Movement or Speech;
I did What little I cou'd do for him
ther & then carry'd him down to the Beach,
& then, the next Day, by easy Stages Home.

Despite my Care for him, he did not regayn
any of thos Powers lost in his Fall;
since Death was certain, I told him of my Plan;
viz., That incertain of *Christian* Buriall,

not having yet been taught by him in this,
but at the same Time, being a *Heathen* no more,
I had som Notions of the Sacrifice
& Ceremony proper to insure

his Souls Release. I thought it for the best
not to belabour this; but meerly to repeat
the Words of his Saviour at the last Feast,
when to his Fellowes, he say'd, *Take ye & eat*

of my owne Flesh in the Remembrance of me;
he seem'd mutch agitated as I spoak
& very pleas'd, as ownly I cou'd see;
but of course, he cou'd say nothing for his Stroak.

XII

Draw a sharp Blade a round the Neck of the Goat
& all 4 Hooves, then make a nother Slyt
with your Knife right at the Base of the Throat
over the Wind-Pipe & then lengthen it,

drawing the Knife down-wards from that Poynt
in a firm Manner, moving down the Breast
& going on untill you come to the Vent;
the Knife Blade shou'd not be too firmly press'd

or the Bagg will rupture, souring the Flesh;
remove the In-sides & scrub owt the Cavity
with Handfulls of twisted Grasses to keep it fresh;
& now the Skin will come off easily,

in 1 single Peece, once the Lymms ha' been slyt
exactly as was mention'd up above;
then work your Blade in betwixt Flesh & Pelt
& peel the latter back-wards like a Glove;

be carefull not to press with the Blade too hard
or you will tear the Pelt; when it's remov'd
use a sharpen'd Shell to scrape a Way the Lard
& Gristle clinging to the In-side; then shave

the Hairs clean off the Out-side; pound to soften
& then stretch it owt to dry in the Sun;
after some Time it will most likely stiffen;
then take it down & pound it once agayn,

softlier this Time; after somemore of this
you will find owt, that in a little While
the Skin of your Goat will mutch resemble his
& may be us'd as Parchment for your Quill.

XIII

Now being my Self entirely a Loan
upon the Island & somewhat at a Loss
for what to do, having so long done
as I was bidden, I waited for his Voice;

and whil I was waiting, I begun to bild
my *Figur Fetisches* a long the Shoar;
and finding that this Occupation fill'd
my Days agreeably, I bilded some more:

When no Ships came, I made up for the Lack
by bilding ı of Drift-wood Scraps & Peeces;
and, as my Shipps wanted Heathens to attack,
I went to wher the Cannibals had feasted;

tho' not withowt considerable Anxiety;
and after picking Care-fully thro' the Sand
I made some whol *Cannibals* from a Variety
of Parts; taking from this ı heer a Hand

and from that ı over ther a broakin Skull
or something els which he no longer needed,
& set them owt to menace my Drift-wood Hull
on Wooden Sticks; after this I added

more Europeans to flesh owt my Crew,
carv'd owt of Wood, with Rifles for Protection;
and then retir'd to admire my *Tableau*,
as tho' I were *God*, after the *Creation*:

How mutch it pleas'd me, to see my Goat Skin Sails
swolne with Breezes; and my Ship lift & plunge
my brave Crew menac'd by *Cannibals*
& my larger Figurs watching from above;

but after a whil I grew troubl'd in Mind,
& my Heart pounded and I was mutch affraid;
for when I look'd, no wher cou'd I find
no Place for *Friday* in what *Friday* made;

then I was suddenly stricken & the Sun
seem'd to fly In-side my poor bursting Skull
& I stumbl'd dizzily a whil & then
fell down the Way that dead Mens Bodys fall.

XIV

Often in Feaver I wou'd cry owt, dreaming
agayn of my Deliverance: I flee
a Mob of Fiends in humane Bodys screaming
lowder than the Sea-Shoars Foam & Sprye;

I run betwicks the Forest & the Ocean,
but burthen'd with my *Masters* Cloaths & Goods,
fatigu'd & ever slower in my Motion
untill I come by that Poynt in the Woods

from which he lept owt to my Assistance
and pass it by   *nowher is my* Master
no wher Delivery   my ownly Chance
of escaping thes Fiends is to run faster

but tho' I run as tho' my Heart wou'd burst
they gain upon me   ther Cries grow lowder
in my Ears   yet even so I durst
throw no Thing off   Bullets   Baskets   Powder-

Horns   the Muskets which I durst not paws
to load & fire   the Pair of Pumps upon
my Feet   my Chequer'd Shirt   my Linnen Draws
either to fling off all or be undone

and I am seiz'd & flung upon my Back
environ'd by Cannibals that pin me down
whil others of them commence to chop & hack:
the Savage Face I look into is mine

no longer   Why, here I am in Bed, unhurt;
by sputtering Candle, see my wooden Chair;
upon it, folded, see my Draws & Shirt;
and all my Phrenzy vanishes into the Nights Air. . . .

Sufficiently recover'd to step owt
the following Morning, I find my Self
puzzl'd, perplex'd, *as in the deepest Doubt;*
standing with my Hand upon the Shelf

next to the Door; upon it, my *Masters* Cloathes
all lay as tho' a waiting his Return
neatly folded. I dress my Self in thes
and take up his Rifle & his Powder-Horn

his Hat & his Umbrella; and so, in his Apparell
I set owt, *as tho' to run a Way from Home;*
what Spirit made me do it, I cannot tell,
nor cou'd I say wher I desir'd to roam,

for it was not I who set owt, nor was it him,
nor was it the both of us to-gether;
I know not who it was; but, as in my Dream
of the Night befor, when I was neither

Master nor *Friday,* but I partook of each,
so it was that Morning. Whatever my Intention
I find my self walking on that Beach
to-wards that Poynt which I have earlier mention'd

and when I pass it by un-harm'd, I collaps
upon the Sand   *I lay ther in great Fear*
for a great long Time   no Savage Shapes
assail mine Eye   no screeching payns mine Ear

Mr Dorrington's Discovery

ca. 1727

A herd of wild Goats having been reported
we putt 2 Boats a Shoar on an uncharted
Island neer the Mowth of the great River
Oroonoko; and there the Men discover'd
a very agreeable yong Savage, attir'd
in a Suit of Goat Skins.
                    When they enquir'd
merrily, *Was Tayloring his Trade,*
he answer'd them in *English: A Planter made*
this Suit for him & other ones besyde;
but now poor he, that since this Planter dy'd
must be his own Taylor.
                Ask'd how he came
to dwell here, *Friday* (for that was the Name
this Planter gave him) told the Men this Tale:
That he was rais'd upon a nother Isle
some Ways from heer; and was a Caribb *Prince;*
that he had liv'd on this Isle ever since
captur'd in War-fare by a Tribe that brought him
heer for a Feast; that being what they thought him;
but he escap'd, and liv'd a great long while
with a mis-fortunate Planter from Brazil
who'd run a Grownd here. For nearly 15 Years
(rows of notched shoots became a wall of spears)
until this Planter dy'd, they liv'd together.
This Planter taught him English, et cetera.
This Evening he spoak of unseen Powers
& rav'd, delerious, for severall Howres.
Beside him lay a Goat Skin-Leather Cape
roughly cut into a Mans own Shape.

Earnestly he begg'd me to examine
this Heathen Fetisch; but an inhumane
Stench assail'd me when I try'd to do it,
for a Multitude of Worms had tunnel'd through it,
as Sappers do, to undermine a City
& left it scribbl'd with their rude *Graffiti*.
I ask'd, *Is this your own Divinity?*
All Things do say O to him, was his reply,
and gave it to me, charging me to keep
it for him safely. With that, he fell a Sleep
and I remov'd my Self, taking his Parcell,
which, as I say, reek'd like the very Devill
and was, no Doubt, the Source of his Feaver.
I gave it to my Man to throw it over-
board and now have some Hope he may recover.

III

Landscape without History

Easter Sunday, 1985

*To take steps toward the reappearance alive of the
disappeared is a subversive act, and measures will be
adopted to deal with it.* —GENERAL OSCAR MEJIA
VICTORES, PRESIDENT OF GUATEMALA

In the Palace of the President this morning,
The General is gripped by the suspicion
That those who were disappeared will be returning
In a subversive act of resurrection.

Why do you worry? The disappeared can never
Be brought back from wherever they were taken;
The age of miracles is gone forever;
These are not sleeping, nor will they awaken.

And if some tell you Christ once reappeared
Alive, one Easter morning, that he was seen—
Give them the lie, for who today can find him?

He is perhaps with those who were disappeared,
Broken and killed, flung into some ravine
With his arms safely wired up behind him.

July 1914

after Anna Akhmatova

I

A stench of burning. For the past four weeks
The peat in the marshes has been smoldering.
The timid aspen bough no longer quakes
At the slightest breeze, the birds no longer sing.

God has abandoned us. We've had no rain
Since Eastertime: the blackened wheat is dead.
A crippled man came into the courtyard once
To prophesy, and this is what he said:

"Horrors approach us—soon the earth will swell
With those who have died of plague and famine;
Earthquakes will open up new paths to hell,
And in the sky strange portents will be seen.

But the brutal invaders cannot destroy
This land entirely—no, they will fail:
God's holy mother will conceal their joy
And our sorrow with a pure white veil. . . . "

II

From burning woods, the smell of juniper.
All throughout the village, despairing wives
And widows weep for the fallen soldiers,
Weep for the children, weep for their own lives.

At last the unrelenting Father yields,
And the crops are drenched. Not at all in vain,
Those prayers of ours: the blackened fields
Run with our blood. We had asked for rain.

Such emptiness. The barren sky descends,
And in the dark one hears a frightened voice:
"O they have numbered Thy most holy wounds,
And for Thy garments they are casting dice. . . . "

III

After the buying, selling, looting and betrayal,
The batlike wing of death led us to where
Anguished jaws were shivering a fleshless skull . . .
Yet what we feel is nothing like despair:

Out of the dark woods close by the town, our days
Are suffused with the scent of wild cherry,
And at night the flickering stars parade
In regiments across the summer sky.

Unutterable holiness bows down
Over the ruins. It was always near,
But we didn't know this, we had never known,
Though we longed from earliest times for it to appear.

"Grace, Secrets, Mysteries . . . "

Fatima, 1917

Three scowling, hamfisted faces
Squint at the alien camera suspiciously:
Lucia, Jacinta and Francisco,
    Monsters of piety

    And self-abasement, fresh
Green shoots grafted to the ancient stem
Of penitence. They mortify their serious flesh
    Until Our Lady must caution them:

    "Drink stale ditchwater, share
Your lunches with poorer children or your sheep;
Enough, no more—my Son is troubled when you wear
    Thick ropes to cut you in your sleep. . . . "

    But what is enough, when nothing
Seems to be? When no amount of suffering suffices
To close the gates of hell?
                Lucia hangs
    Above the agonizing faces

    Of the damned, a scum of souls
Weightlessly drifting on a sea of fire.
What is enough? Demons rake the coals
    And waves of flame leap higher.

    But who will heed the warning
Of these devout, uneducated children?
Only those who are themselves already burning
    In the earth's slow cauldron,

Gnarled as the olives and scrub oaks
That have learned to live almost without water
In the meager hills where every pile of rocks
    Commemorates its virgin martyr—

Attacked, of course, by the atheist
Mayor, whose strident printing press bids faction
Unite with faction: "REPUBLICANS! Awaken and resist
    The seductive music of reaction!"

The Great War widens and Portugal
Begins to slide: conscripts herded first to Mass,
Then to the trenches. Lucia's twin cousins inhale
    Barbed hooks of mustard gas,

Return to proclaim that the scattered
Innocents of every explosion
Limb by luckless limb will be regathered
    On the Day of Resurrection;

And at Lourdes, Anatole France,
"Quaffing the cynic's cup to the last, bitter dregs,"
Faced with a long wallful of jettisoned crutches and canes,
    Asked, "What—are there no wooden legs?"

Mandelstam in Transit

My age, my beast, is there one who
Will lift his head to meet your stare,
Or with his living blood repair
That fractured spine of yours for you?
Long years of suffering. Now this:
A spineless, parasitic crew
Herding us on toward the abyss.

Until he's finished in his grave,
As long as he has breath, a man
Must feel, above his covered spine,
A gentle rippling, like a wave.
But now the tender cartilage
Of childhood is broken, the crown
Of first life crushed in pointless rage.

For life at last to break away,
For the new world to take root,
The hollow music of the flute
Must link up each disjointed day.
But the age is troubled by its dreams:
A serpent winding underfoot
Hisses the true music of the times.

Green shoots, my age, will once again
Rise up, new buds will once more swell,
My pitied dear, my beautiful,
Despite your agonizing pain—
What lies in your deceitful smile!
You turn back, staring at the stain
Of blood on snow, mile after mile.

Landscape without History

I EARLY MORNING AT HARTWELL POND, VERMONT

Finding in the trap by the kitchen table
An ounce or so of mouse, with one eye closed
And one incongruously made of blood,
I set out juice, milk, two kinds of cereal
—But not, of course before having first disposed
Of this one, from whom the mountains of our food
Were kept by a tiny piece of bacon;
A morsel that snapped back as it was taken
Cruelly pinned that ruby to its eye
And crushed its snout and snuffed its fingertips. . . .
After I wash my hands of the beast
I turn to the stove: now eggs begin to fry
In sweet butter, now the coffee drips:
I call my children down to share this feast.

II At the Museum in St. Johnsbury

In the museum at St. Johnsbury
A split stump and its colony of mice
Have been re-created as a freeze-dried
Diorama: motionless rodents scurry
About in a simulated busyness,
Doing what they were doing when they died,
Or just before—which is, of course, not so:
They're part of an arrangement, a tableau,
All caught up in a moment from which there
Was no appeal

                      ancient figures of Pompeii
         immobilized two thousand years ago

         their cries left hanging in the smoky air

         all but their last gestures burned away
         under the warm and suffocating snow

III Composition with Rocks and Grasses

Glacial action chiseled this arrangement
Of three pieces of shale as an afterthought
To the real work of gouging the pond itself.
That ice raised no imposing monument
But slid away until these steps were cut
Out of the pond's steeply descending shelf
And tilted up.
                    Another arrangement made
With local grasses provided stem and blade,
Yielding diagonals that comb the three
Slabs of grey bedrock with strands of gold and green
To soften the severity of the composition
And introduce a new complexity
As time flows through the spaces in between
The quickened rocks that now reflect each season.

When I first hear, then sight, the possibly
Armed fighter streaking overhead, I wonder
Absently whether it's just another dress
Rehearsal, or the thing itself, finally.
As usual, for practice, I surrender
Myself and the ones I love as hostages
To the whining echoes of its aftermath.
I have rehearsed surrender in the path
Of our once-flung, inexorable weapons
Often enough, while some finger paused between
Go back home to base, go on to megakill—

Blips on a screen. Our helplessness sharpens
The shark's tooth against us, as against the green
Wall at the pond's back, now quivering, now still.

To the Living Bait

The hook is now firmly embedded between your shoulder-
    blades: that was the sharp pain you may have felt just
    a moment ago.
Your hands and feet will feel a little bit colder,
    But there should be no pain at all now. Please signal
    if there is pain. No?

Good. Then let us continue. At our first session
    Together, you brought up those questions we've come
    to expect:
"Why am I here? Why should I have been chosen?"
    By now you will have had more than sufficient time to
    reflect

On our responses, which ranged from the artfully shaded
    Moderately evasive equivocation to the openfaced,
    outright lie.
"There was no reason at all," you will have concluded,
    "It was an accident that brought me here." Please
    signal if you disagree.

No, nothing required that you should have been lifted
    Out of the flow and not someone else. For if we had
    needed to use
Someone clever or goodlooking or in any way gifted,
    We would have left you at home in bed, watching the
    evening news,

Since you weren't any of those things ever,
	Were you? And if you had been, that too would be
	perfectly fine,
Though you would be thinking, "Because I am clever
	Or gifted or handsome, I find myself here at the end
	of the line."

Not so. For nothing more is ever required
	Of those, like yourself, who advance to the final
	selection
Than a perfectly normal need to be desired
	And an equally normal, even commendable, fear of
	rejection.

These suit you, briefly, to our purpose. Which is
	Merely to learn if anything under the surface might be
	so provoked
To anger or hunger by your insensible twitches
	That it will answer your need with its own, and find
	itself hooked.

Are you ready now? Please don't bother replying.
	Thanks to you, so far, everything has gone just as we
	planned.
This will not comfort you while you are dying.
	Don't think we don't understand.

Making Faces

for Peter Schumann

We begin to see that it is better to keep life fluid and
changing than to try to hold it down fast in heavy
monuments. . . . Give us things that are alive and flexible,
which won't last too long and become an obstruction and a
weariness. —D. H. LAWRENCE

I THE WORLD

Every year there is a big parade
In Barton, Vermont, on the Fourth of July
When we celebrate the red white and blue—
During the course of which we see displayed
Some of the Pentagon's old weaponry;
An armored car, a Sherman tank or two
Add martial tone to the festive atmosphere:
Behind them come the Bread & Puppet Theatre,
Beginning with someone in a horse's head
Who's holding up a sign which says, THE WORLD,
As though the world were next in their procession,
Or their procession were the world instead.
And next to the horse there walks a little girl
Ringing a schoolbell for our attention:

The world we see approaching is a cart
Drawn by puppet oxen, their huge necks bent,
Their tranquil heads sweeping from side to side;
The world is filled with artless works of art,
Miniature figures that must represent
The people of the world out for a ride.
And the cart so full of them that one might say
No one at all has been left home today.
The world has drawn beside us now and soon
Will pass us by as the clouds pass us by
Overhead. The clouds move at their own pace
And so to us they hardly seem to move,
Those ghostly, gray-white oxen of the sky
Drawing the world through realms of empty space.

This world addresses the fragility
Of the only other one we have to live in,
Where the marble-breasted laborers grow weak
And stumble to their knees and shortly die;
Where the poor must eat the stones that they are given
And the little painted figures fall and break;
And the extraordinary cloud-drawn cart
We thought would last forever comes apart.
What happens next in the parade, we ask?
We haven't long to wait before our answer:
Behind the cart drawn by the puppet oxen
Comes a stilted figure in a jackal's mask,
Pounding on a drum! This dog-faced dancer
Raises a clangorous, dissonant tocsin:

II THE END OF THE WORLD

We've practiced it too often in our age
To see it merely as the subtraction
Of bird from tree, of tree from earth, of earth from space,
As one erases letters from a page.
Yet we still think of it as an abstraction,
Something that isn't likely to take place—
Although it's taken place at places called
Guernica, Hiroshima, Buchenwald.
We think of the unthinkable with ease,
We've had such practice of it for so long;
And speak of it in ways which help conceal
From ourselves the dark realities
That numb the mind and paralyze the tongue.
And now in the parade there comes a skel-

etal figure on a skeletal horse,
Made of raw strips of pine lashed together.
Its attitude is distant yet familiar,
As though it were confident that in the course
Of time we'd get to know each other better.
It knows this in its bones, as we in ours.
(And so if Death should ever wave at you,
You may wave back, for you have manners too;
You needn't ask it to slow down or stop.)
It's followed by a Dragon, belching smoke;
One Demon drives it, another one attends
To the Great Devourer who sits on top,
Quietly enjoying some huge cosmic joke—
And that is the way The End Of The World ends.

III   Fɪɢʜᴛ ᴛʜᴇ Eɴᴅ ᴏғ ᴛʜᴇ Wᴏʀʟᴅ

Now Peter Schumann, dressed as Uncle Sam,
Strides down Main Street on his outrageous stilts
Carrying a sign that says, ᴡᴀᴛᴄʜ ᴏᴜᴛ!
A younger Uncle Sam prances around him,
Intricately weaving subtle steps
Under his teacher's exaggerated strut—
"They make it look so easy," someone says.
They dance before a ragtime band which plays
Molto con brio, more or less on key;
For there are many fine musicians in it
And they raise a joyful noise unto the Lord
Of all creation. The heart willingly
Gives its assent, but mind says, Wait a minute—
Is this now we're to Fight The End Of The World?

—By making faces at appalling forces
And marching off to the Parade Grounds with
One's friends and neighbors, honest country folk
Changed into demons, dogs and demi-horses,
Or into oxen who present the world as myth,
Straining together underneath their yoke?
—By building things so that they cannot last
Unreasonably long? By honoring the past,
But raising up no wearisome immense
Rock for all ages? By rudely waking
The child-in-us and teaching it to play?
By going with the grain and not against?
By shaping our daily bread and baking
Thick-crusted loaves of it to give away?

We've seen The World as it was passing through,
And monstrous Death the world-devouring,
And a man on stilts, whose artistry astounded;
And now we have a sanitation crew
Sweeping and shoveling up dragon dung,
Leaving the street as spotless as they'd found it.
My questions beg an answer, as do I.
Some kind of answer may be given by
The Garbageman who shakes hands with my son
And daughter, then goes back to join his friends;
Or the Washerwoman in her faded dress,
On a holiday from work that's never done,
With whom, most fittingly, the pageant ends:
As she passes by, her sign says only, YES

Steal the Bacon

Designed by Ann Walston.

Composed by Brushwood Graphics, Inc., in Palatino.

Printed by Thomson-Shore, Inc.,
on 60-lb. Glatfelter Offset text.